My first day of school
E Sco   158802

Wilton Public Library

DATE DUE			
WDC			

Wilton Public Library
1215 Cypress Street
P.O. Box 447
Wilton, IA 52778

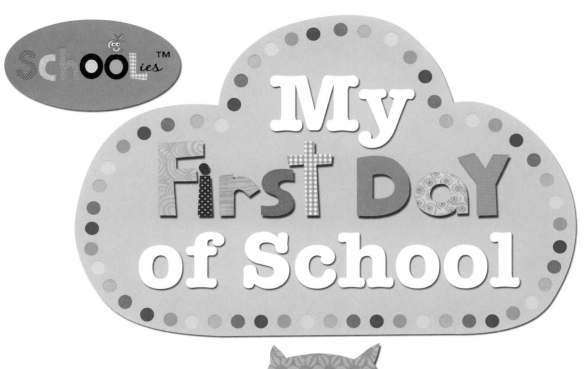

My First Day of School

Based on the characters created by
Ellen Crimi-Trent

priddy books

When Spencer woke up,
he had a fluttery thought.

Spencer's tummy flipped and flopped.
He went to see his mom.

Spencer's feathers ruffled.
He went to see his big brother, Colby.

Spencer's ears twitched.
He put on his roller skates
and felt a little better.

Mr. Mouse drove up in the school bus.
Spencer's wings flapped fearfully.

Spencer hopped on the bus
and looked around.

Spencer saw friendly faces
smiling at him.

Spencer's ears didn't twitch.
His stomach didn't flip or flop.
His wings flapped a little, but he smiled.

At school, their teacher Mrs. Meow
was waiting for them.

She led the Schoolies inside to
their classroom.

In the classroom, Spencer sat beside Hayden Hoot.

Right away, Mrs. Meow taught
the Schoolies new things.

Spencer's ears twitched again.
But soon he was counting along with
Hayden, who really loved math!

Then, Mrs. Meow taught them the letters of the alphabet.

At recess time,
the Schoolies played outside.

Spencer was really having fun now!

At lunch time, Spencer's tummy rumbled.

There was lots of good food to eat.
Spencer ate a sandwich and some fruit,
and he drank up all his milk.

Then came story time. Mrs. Meow read
a story about her first day of school.
It was Spencer's favorite part of the day.

Too soon, it was time to go home.
Spencer's feathers drooped.
He would miss all his new friends.

Goodbye!

TOOT!

TOOT!

Mr. Mouse drove
the Schoolies home

Back at home, Spencer told his mom every new thing that had happened at school.

Spencer had a fluttery thought.